SEATTLE PUBLIC LIBRARY

# SPORTS GREAT KEVIN GARNETT

# —Sports Great Books—

## BASEBALL
Sports Great Jim Abbott
0-89490-395-0/ Savage
Sports Great Bobby Bonilla
0-89490-417-5/ Knapp
Sports Great Ken Griffey, Jr.
0-7660-1266-2/ Savage
Sports Great Orel Hershiser
0-89490-389-6/ Knapp
Sports Great Bo Jackson
0-89490-281-4/ Knapp
Sports Great Greg Maddux
0-89490-873-1/ Thornley
Sports Great Kirby Puckett
0-89490-392-6/ Aaseng
Sports Great Cal Ripken, Jr.
0-89490-387-X/ Macnow
Sports Great Nolan Ryan
0-89490-394-2/ Lace
Sports Great Darryl Strawberry
0-89490-291-1/ Torres & Sullivan
Sports Great Frank Thomas
0-7660-1269-7/ Deane

## BASKETBALL
Sports Great Charles Barkley
(Revised Edition)
0-7660-1004-X/ Macnow
Sports Great Larry Bird
0-89490-368-3/ Kavanagh
Sports Great Kobe Bryant
0-7660-1264-6/ Macnow
Sports Great Muggsy Bogues
0-89490-876-6/ Rekela
Sports Great Patrick Ewing
0-89490-369-1/ Kavanagh
Sports Great Kevin Garnett
0-7660-1263-8/ Macnow
Sports Great Anfernee Hardaway
0-89490-758-1/ Rekela
Sports Great Juwan Howard
0-7660-1065-1/ Savage
Sports Great Magic Johnson
(Revised and Expanded)
0-89490-348-9/ Haskins
Sports Great Michael Jordan
(Revised Edition)
0-89490-978-9/ Aaseng
Sports Great Jason Kidd
0-7660-1001-5/ Torres
Sports Great Karl Malone
0-89490-599-6/ Savage
Sports Great Reggie Miller
0-89490-874-X/ Thornley
Sports Great Alonzo Mourning
0-89490-875-8/ Fortunato
Sports Great Dikembe Mutombo
0-7660-1267-0/ Torres
Sports Great Shaquille O'Neal
(Revised Edition)
0-7660-1003-1/ Sullivan

Sports Great Scottie Pippen
0-89490-755-7/ Bjarkman
Sports Great Mitch Richmond
0-7660-1070-8/ Grody
Sports Great David Robinson
(Revised Edition)
0-7660-1077-5/ Aaseng
Sports Great Dennis Rodman
0-89490-759-X/ Thornley
Sports Great John Stockton
0-89490-598-8/ Aaseng
Sports Great Isiah Thomas
0-89490-374-8/ Knapp
Sports Great Chris Webber
0-7660-1069-4/ Macnow
Sports Great Dominique Wilkins
0-89490-754-9/ Bjarkman

## FOOTBALL
Sports Great Troy Aikman
0-89490-593-7/ Macnow
Sports Great Jerome Bettis
0-89490-872-3/ Majewski
Sports Great John Elway
0-89490-282-2/ Fox
Sports Great Brett Favre
0-7660-1000-7/ Savage
Sports Great Jim Kelly
0-89490-670-4/ Harrington
Sports Great Joe Montana
0-89490-371-3/ Kavanagh
Sports Great Jerry Rice
0-89490-419-1/ Dickey
Sports Great Barry Sanders
(Revised Edition)
0-7660-1067-8/ Knapp
Sports Great Deion Sanders
0-7660-1068-6/ Macnow
Sports Great Emmitt Smith
0-7660-1002-3/ Grabowski
Sports Great Herschel Walker
0-89490-207-5/ Benagh

## OTHER
Sports Great Michael Chang
0-7660-1223-9/ Ditchfield
Sports Great Oscar De La Hoya
0-7660-1066-X/ Torres
Sports Great Steffi Graf
0-89490-597-X/ Knapp
Sports Great Wayne Gretzky
0-89490-757-3/ Rappoport
Sports Great Mario Lemieux
0-89490-596-1/ Knapp
Sports Great Eric Lindros
0-89490-871-5/ Rappoport
Sports Great Pete Sampras
0-89490-756-5/ Sherrow

# SPORTS GREAT KEVIN GARNETT

Glen Macnow

—*Sports Great Books*—

 **Enslow Publishers, Inc.**
40 Industrial Road     PO Box 38
Box 398     Aldershot
Berkeley Heights, NJ 07922     Hants GU12 6BP
USA     UK
http://www.enslow.com

*To my son, Alex. Like Kevin Garnett, you are a
great young talent and a hard worker*

Copyright © 2000 by Glen Macnow.

All rights reserved.

No part of this book may be reproduced by any means
without the written permission of the publisher.

**Library of Congress Cataloging-in-Publication Data**

Macnow, Glen.
    Sports great Kevin Garnett / Glen Macnow.
       p. cm. — (Sports great books)
    Includes bibliographical references and index.
    Summary: Follows the basketball career of the popular Minnesota Timberwolves
forward who, in 1997, signed the largest contract in the history of pro sports.
    ISBN 0-7660-1263-8
    1. Garnett, Kevin, 1976– —Juvenile literature. 2. Basketball players—United
States Biography Juvenile literature. [1. Garnett, Kevin, 1976– . 2. Basketball
players. 3. Afro-Americans Biography.] I. Title. II. Title: Kevin Garnett. III. Series.
GV884.G37M23 2000
796.323'092—dc21
[B]                                                                                                             99-40390
                                                                                                                 CIP

Printed in the United States of America

10 9 8 7 6 5 4 3 2 1

**To Our Readers:**
All Internet addresses in this book were active and appropriate when we went to press. Any
comments or suggestions can be sent by e-mail to Comments@enslow.com or to the address
on the back cover.

**Illustration Credits:** Andrew D. Bernstein/NBA Photos, p. 48; Barry Gossage/
NBA Photos, p. 27; Bill Baptist/NBA Photos, p. 8; David Sherman/NBA Photos,
pp. 18, 45, 50; Glenn James/NBA Photos, p. 36; John Grieshop/NBA Photos, p. 32;
Lou Capozzola/NBA Photos, p. 59; Nathaniel S. Butler/NBA Photos, pp. 12, 14, 23;
Noren Trotman/NBA Photos, pp. 53, 55, 57; Sam Forencich/NBA Photos, p. 39;
Scott Cunningham/NBA Photos, p. 21; Tim Defrisco/NBA Photos, pp. 30, 41.

**Cover Illustration:** Sam Forencich/NBA Photos.

# *Contents*

*Chapter 1* . . . . . . . . . . . . . . . . . . . . . . . . . . . 7

*Chapter 2* . . . . . . . . . . . . . . . . . . . . . . . . . . 16

*Chapter 3* . . . . . . . . . . . . . . . . . . . . . . . . . . 25

*Chapter 4* . . . . . . . . . . . . . . . . . . . . . . . . . . 34

*Chapter 5* . . . . . . . . . . . . . . . . . . . . . . . . . . 43

*Chapter 6* . . . . . . . . . . . . . . . . . . . . . . . . . . 52

   *Career Statistics* . . . . . . . . . . . . . . . . . . . . . . 61

   *Where to Write* . . . . . . . . . . . . . . . . . . . . . . 62

   *Index* . . . . . . . . . . . . . . . . . . . . . . . . . . . . . 63

# Chapter 1

The six-foot eleven-inch forward—rail thin and as fast as running water—swooped across the lane. He curled the basketball under his arm. He paused, just for a split second, to plan his next move.

Kevin Garnett looked at the men covering him for the Phoenix Suns: There was Charles Barkley, an old warhorse, tough and experienced. There was Kevin Johnson, quick and smart, making a move to steal the ball from Garnett's grasp. There was Danny Manning, a solid defensive player, hanging near the basket to stop Garnett from driving.

Garnett started his dribble. He pushed the ball to his left, getting Johnson to grab for it. But Garnett then quickly shifted the ball to his right, and Johnson grabbed only air.

With a stutter-step, Garnett got Barkley back on his heels. Then the younger, quicker Garnett drove by, showing little respect for the great Sir Charles.

Only Manning now stood between Kevin Garnett and two points. As he headed toward the net, Garnett leaped. Manning reached out to block the shot. But Garnett, in midair, twisted

Basketball great Charles Barkley can only watch as Kevin Garnett rises above the rim. Even as an inexperienced nineteen-year-old rookie, Garnett was making a strong impression on opponents and fans.

under Manning's tree-limb-like arm. Still flying forward, Garnett sailed past the basket. Just before he returned to earth, he softly tossed the ball over his right shoulder. It kissed off the glass and swished through the net.

Basket. It was only worth two points, but it spoke volumes.

Kevin Garnett was just nineteen years old at the time, but as a rookie forward for the Minnesota Timberwolves, he took three of the National Basketball Association's biggest stars to school on one play. The Phoenix Suns won that game in January 1996, but it was Garnett, then a rookie, whom the fans went home talking about. The words they used to describe him—"incredible," "unbelievable," "Jordan-like"—are the words reserved only for superstars in waiting.

At an age when most teenagers are only dreaming of their futures, Kevin Garnett was living his. At an age when most young men are studying or just starting their careers, Garnett was already near the top of his profession.

He joined the National Basketball Association (NBA) right out of high school. At the time, most experts thought he had made the wrong choice. Skipping college, they said, meant he was jumping in competition, from playing against the best kids in the neighborhood to playing against the best athletes in the world. Nobody can jump that many levels. He needed time to grow, they said, in his game if not physically.

Besides, they said, what business did a teenager have running in the NBA? He could not be expected to handle the pressures of adult life. Pro ball is a business, not just a game. What does a kid know about being in a business? And how would a teenager handle the temptations, the boredom, the sink-or-swim lifestyle that professional athletes have to deal with? Very few players had successfully made the jump from high school to pro ball. In fact, those issues have caused older men to fail in the NBA. Garnett was just barely old enough to vote.

It turned out that Garnett could handle himself with the older guys. He was both a good kid and a great talent. This is what some of his elders said about Kevin Garnett.

NBA Hall of Famer Magic Johnson: "I see a little bit of me in him when I was his age, except that I couldn't jump that high and I certainly wasn't blocking any shots. The NBA has all these guys they're pushing. The guy they should be pushing is Kevin Garnett. He's one of the guys that will take the league to the next level."

Charles Barkley: "He can be as good as he wants to be. He's got tremendous talent and a great body. Those long arms help him a lot. And his head is certainly screwed on straight. I don't think he'll ever turn into a knucklehead."

Timberwolves general manager Kevin McHale, also a Hall of Famer: "If KG were only six-feet-six or six-feet-seven instead of six-feet-eleven, he would still be a great player. He's a physical freak. And I mean that in a good way."

In his first four seasons, Garnett—known as Da Kid, or KG—established himself as one of pro basketball's rising talents. He has a combination of size, skills, enthusiasm, and personality that quickly put him in the center ring of NBA stars.

During his first four years his numbers improved every season. He averaged 10.4 points per game as a rookie. That is not a bad number, but it is nothing spectacular. He increased his average to 17.0 points in his second season, then to 18.5 in his third. By his fourth season he was scoring more than 20 points per game.

But what makes Garnett more valuable is his versatility—that is, his ability to do many things well. In his third year, 1997–98, he finished tenth in the NBA in rebounds. He was also the only player among more than four hundred in the league to finish in the top twenty-five in rebounding, scoring, assists, blocks, steals, and minutes played. There seemed to be no weakness in his game.

Minnesota fans recognized that special talent. Not only was Garnett named the Timberwolves' Most Valuable Player (MVP) two years in a row; he was also voted by fans as the most popular player on the team.

In fact, fans around the NBA quickly caught on to this rising star. Garnett made the 1997 NBA All-Star Game as a substitute, chosen by the coaches. The next year, when he was just twenty-one years old, he was voted by millions of fans across the nation to start for the Western Conference team. Garnett used the trip to New York City's Madison Square Garden as a learning tool. He asked every player who would answer him how he could improve his game. That, he said, was his way of going to school.

The Timberwolves also knew how talented and dedicated their young leader was. Out of high school, Garnett received a three-year contract that paid him $5.6 million. That is amazing money for anyone, let alone a nineteen-year-old.

But his next contract was beyond amazing; it was unbelievable. After three seasons in Minnesota, Garnett could become a free agent. That meant he could sign with any team he wanted to. In order to avoid losing him, the Timberwolves offered him the largest contract in sports history. The team would pay Garnett a whopping $125 million over six years. The Timberwolves agreed to pay the money, not so much because of what Garnett had already done, but because of what management believed he could do. The Wolves believed that Garnett would emerge as one of the NBA's superstars, reach the heights of Magic Johnson or Michael Jordan, and carry the team to a championship.

Garnett's greatest asset is his ability to do many things very well. In his third season, he was the only player in the league to finish in the top twenty-five in rebounding, scoring, assists, blocks, steals, and minutes played.

The contract sent shock waves through the league. Many NBA owners were alarmed that a player so young could make so much money. In fact, the league shut down for the first two months of the 1998–99 season while owners and players fought over money. Nothing was more responsible for the shutdown than owners' anger over Garnett's paycheck.

For his part, Garnett was not much affected by the huge contract. He still shopped at the mall with everyone else. He still dined on fast food, although he tried to stick with a healthy diet. His spare time was spent playing video games and listening to CDs, or watching basketball on tapes and satellite TV. His one present to himself was a yellow Range Rover, which friends called the Bus. When you are a six-foot eleven-inch man, driving a big truck seems to make sense.

Recently, Garnett's interests have started branching out. He made a movie, *Rebound*, in which he played basketball legend Wilt Chamberlain. He started a line of clothing with some friends. And he started taking college courses. He wanted to learn how to handle his money.

Mostly, he focused on his first love—basketball. Garnett is often compared with San Antonio Spurs star David Robinson, because he can do so many things on the floor and is so graceful doing them. But Robinson is a true center. Garnett, tall as he is, is a natural small forward.

Actually, he is capable of playing all five positions. Envision a bigger Penny Hardaway, a faster Magic Johnson, a quicker Chris Webber, a more versatile Dikembe Mutombo, and a more mobile Shaquille O'Neal. "Kevin is the best twenty-two-year-old in the world," his Timberwolves coach, Flip Saunders, said in 1999. "He is also our leader. If everyone in the world worked as hard at what they do as Kevin does, we would all be better off."

The day that Saunders made those statements, Garnett

Garnett was all smiles after the Timberwolves signed him to a six-year, $125 million-dollar contract.

had led his teammates through a two-hour practice. The Timberwolves had lost the night before, and Garnett was angry at their lack of effort. When practice ended, Garnett stayed late. Just he and a ball boy were left in the gym.

For an hour, Garnett practiced foul shots. He did not stop until he made fifty in a row. Then he worked on a sky hook, which he was hoping to add to his arsenal. He asked the ball boy, who was not even six feet tall, to stand in a spot on the court where an opponent might try to block his shot. Then Garnett launched sky hook after sky hook, until he felt he had made some progress that day.

Finally he left the court. Sweat dripped from his face. According to his coach, Garnett was the best twenty-two-year-old player in the world. He himself would not be satisfied until he was the best player of any age.

The funny thing is that if Kevin Garnett's mother had it her way, he would not be playing basketball at all.

# Chapter 2

Kevin Maurice Garnett was born May 19, 1976, in Greenville, South Carolina. His mother, Shirley Garnett, was a deeply religious and very serious woman. She saw basketball and other sports as foolishness. She wanted Kevin to go to college and become a social worker.

Kevin's parents never married. When Kevin was five, his mother married a man named Ernest Irby. By this time, the family included Kevin's two younger sisters. They moved to Mauldin, South Carolina, a nice, quiet town of brick houses and tall trees.

Childhood friends remember Kevin as someone who had a basketball in his hands from sunup to sundown. In the summer, most of Kevin's friends would sleep late into the morning. But he loved basketball too much to spend the daylight hours in slumber. He would arise at 6:00 A.M. to hit the local courts.

Kevin and his stepfather did not get along well. Mr. Irby disapproved so much of his stepson's love of basketball that he would not let Kevin post a hoop in his driveway.

One of Kevin's childhood friends, Baron Franks, said Kevin was always a happy-go-lucky kid—except around his stepfather. "Every time I saw him with his stepfather, it was like walking on eggshells," Franks recalled.

Basketball served as Kevin's getaway. "When he was lonely, he grabbed that ball," Franks said. "When he wanted to get out of the house, get away and not think about some things, he played ball."

To some extent, the game is in Kevin's blood. His birth father, O'Lewis McCullough, was once captain of the local high school team. He earned the nickname Bye Bye because on the fast break, he would be gone. Kevin and his dad did not have much contact as Kevin grew up, but they certainly did share a love of basketball.

Because he knew how his mother felt about basketball, Kevin did not tell her that he had tried out for the Mauldin Mavericks early in his freshman year at Mauldin High. In fact, she did not discover he made the team until a month into the season.

Mavericks coach Duke Fisher said that Kevin's mother's disapproval actually fueled him to play better. It seemed that Kevin wanted to prove to her that the sport was not a waste of time if he could become great at it.

"I would bust him at basketball practice, I mean really bust him," Fisher said. "Then he would go to the park and play more basketball there. He would leave one practice and go practice again. I never saw someone so obsessed."

As a freshman, Kevin played for the junior varsity team. He averaged 12.5 points, 14 rebounds, and 7 blocked shots per game. He was already six feet five inches tall, and growing so fast that sometimes he complained that his bones hurt. He was also a bit uncomfortable with his quickly growing body. Sometimes he would trip over his feet, which seemed to be

Kevin's mother, Shirley Garnett, had no idea that her son would play basketball for a living. When he was younger, she wanted him to go to college and become a social worker.

growing a shoe size each month. Other kids teased him because he could not dunk the ball, even though he was the tallest player in the school.

But Kevin was not discouraged. He worked hard for Coach Fisher, who pushed him to work even harder. By the tenth grade, he had made the varsity team and was becoming a leader among the students.

He was also somewhat of a clown. Kevin was always laughing, wrestling, and kidding around. When he dunked the ball (which he learned to do as a sophomore), he would open his mouth and yell on the way down. Coach Fisher had to explain to other coaches that Kevin was not trying to bother or embarrass anyone. He was just having fun. When the high school basketball season ended, Kevin wanted to keep playing. He joined an Amateur Athletic Union (AAU) team, which competed in local teen tournaments and summer league programs. The team, coached by Darren Gazaway, was one of the best in the Carolinas and Kentucky area for more than fifteen years. In fact, when Kevin joined in 1992, seven members of the squad were the MVPs at their high schools. It gave Kevin a chance to play with and learn from the best.

Soon, however, Kevin himself was the best. The kid had good hands and good feet. He was quick and always in position. His instincts—which let him know where the ball was headed—were terrific.

"Kevin could have averaged 30 points a game—easy," Gazaway said. "But he didn't. He averaged about 18 points. He would pass, set up other players. He was not stingy. Just loved to play the game."

He loved it all, except for the free throws. Gazaway spent a lot of time with Kevin on foul shots. He had to get Kevin to settle down and concentrate. "It was almost like he was too hyper to take the time for the throw, like he was thinking, 'Let's get this over with so we can play,'" Gazaway recalled.

By Kevin's junior year in high school, tickets to Mauldin Mavericks games were always sold out. People stood in hallways outside the gym just to listen to Kevin play. He was still growing and now stood at six feet ten inches tall. He averaged 27 points, 17 rebounds, and 7 blocks per game.

By now college coaches and scouts were coming around to watch him play. The biggest universities in the country were interested in star players like Kevin, who could help them win games and draw crowds. Kevin had not given much thought to college. He just knew he wanted to play professional basketball. His mother certainly wanted him to go to college. She still hoped he would consider becoming a social worker so that he could help other people with their problems.

Kevin received a lot of mail at the high school from college coaches. He asked his history teacher, Janie Willoughby, to help him sort through all the letters and postcards. She set aside a large drawer in her desk as Kevin's mailbox and then had to add a second drawer as the letters kept pouring in. Ms. Willoughby also kept a stash of candy bars in the drawer. Kevin was always hungry.

Kevin was a good student in Ms. Willoughby's class. If you told him something, she said, he would never forget it. But reading was tough for him. He struggled with books and got frustrated working with tutors. His teachers warned Kevin that if he did not work harder on his reading, colleges would lose interest in him.

Still, all appeared to be going well for Kevin at Mauldin High. Then something happened to change all that in May 1994, late in his junior year.

What happened that day is something Kevin has never talked about in public. It is something that people who

Garnett developed his basketball skills, including a solid jumper, by spending countless hours on the court when he was a child.

know him find difficult to believe. But it changed Kevin's life forever.

This much is clear: There was a fight in Mauldin High School between one white student from another school and a group of black students from Mauldin. Some witnesses said that the white student started it by hurling racial insults at the black students. Others said that Kevin did nothing more than watch the action. The fight ended with the white student breaking his ankle.

When the police showed up, Kevin was accused of being a participant. He was arrested and taken to the police station. He was in tears when his mother arrived.

Kevin insisted he was not involved, but he and four other students were charged with assault. His arrest made headlines in the local newspapers. Murray Long, a white student who played with Kevin on the Mauldin team, said, "Just knowing Kevin like I do, I don't think he ever would do anything to hurt anyone. And I never understood why the whole thing was made such a big deal."

Eventually the charges were dropped when Kevin and the others agreed to undergo counseling and do volunteer work. Still, Kevin was hurt. He felt abandoned by his coach and many classmates whom he had considered friends. They did not seem to believe his claims of innocence.

Kevin felt at the time that he had only two friends left in the world. One was a neighborhood pal called Jaime "Bug" Peters. The other was Stephon Marbury, a high school player from New York City whom Kevin had never met; they had only spoken over the phone.

A few years later, Garnett and Marbury would be teammates with the Minnesota Timberwolves, but for now, they were just mutual admirers. They knew each other because Kevin had seen Stephon on an ABC-TV *Nightline* show about

Although he is thin for an NBA big man, Garnett is a very strong player. Michael Olowokandi of the Los Angeles Clippers looks as if he has found this out for himself.

prep stars, and also had read a diary Stephon wrote for *Slam* magazine. Stephon had seen Kevin on an ESPN-TV report. One night when Stephon was fifteen and Kevin was sixteen, Stephon called up Kevin out of the blue. They kept on calling each other. The phone bills were eighty dollars a month.

"They must have thought it was a local call," joked Shirley Garnett Irby, Kevin's mom. "Stephon was a real inspiration in Kevin's life. Stephon served as a listener, someone who was there for Kevin in a tough time. Stephon was the one telling Kevin he had to work hard, academically and athletically."

By this time, Mrs. Irby had come to support Kevin's goal to play pro basketball. She knew that his future in Mauldin was over, so she came to a daring decision.

The family would have to pick up and move.

# Chapter 3

After the fight and the arrest, Kevin was not eager to return to Mauldin High. His mother knew they would have to move away so he could get a fresh start. But where?

The answer came from William Nelson, one of Kevin's coaches in a basketball summer camp. Nelson was also the coach at Farragut Academy, a public high school on Chicago's West Side. Farragut Academy's basketball program was regarded as one of the best in the country. Coach Nelson said he would be thrilled to have Kevin play for the school.

So Kevin, his sister Ashley, and his mother packed all their possessions into a station wagon and a trailer and headed for Chicago. His stepfather and another sister stayed back in South Carolina.

In South Carolina, the family had lived in a good-sized house in a nice neighborhood. But in Chicago, their money did not go that far. The three moved into a cramped one-bedroom apartment, which cost seven hundred dollars a month, in a giant complex near the Chicago Medical Center. Kevin's mother took two jobs to support the family. Still, she said, some nights the dinners were beans and rice and nothing more.

"It was hard, very hard, to go to the grocery store and realize you have only $20 to spend," she said. "It was hard having to walk when my car was stolen several times. I cried many nights."

It was tough for Kevin, too. He was not as free to go out and play basketball in Chicago as he had been in Mauldin. Gyms were more likely to be occupied. Not all the courts were safe late at night.

In South Carolina, Kevin had felt safe, at least until the fight and arrest in his junior year. In Chicago, he felt unsure and unsafe. The city was so big and full of strangers. The neighborhood around his apartment complex was polluted by gang members who sold drugs. There were junkies who robbed people to support their habits. Kevin felt lost and scared. Even at school things were tough. Farragut Academy's student body was 90 percent Hispanic American, and relations between Hispanic-American and African-American students were not very good.

"My year in Chicago was total hell—gangs, guns, crime," he later said. "I had to deal with a gang leader named Seven-Gun Marcello. No fun."

He kept up his spirits through chats with his long-distance friend, Stephon Marbury. And despite the troubles around him—or maybe because of them—he increased his focus on basketball.

During his senior season, Kevin blossomed into the great player that many experts thought he could become. He had reached his full height of six feet eleven inches. Still, he had the grace and ball-handling skills of a player seven inches shorter.

In one memorable game that season, Kevin came down

Garnett launches a shot over Rex Chapman of the Phoenix Suns. After having some personal problems in South Carolina, Garnett, his sister Ashley, and his mother moved to Chicago, where he starred at Farragut Academy.

with a defensive rebound and looked to pass off to one of his guards. But the opposing team trapped Farragut's two guards, daring Kevin to move the ball himself. So he did, dribbling between two defenders, heading all the way downcourt, and finishing with a monster dunk. As the crowd was still cheering in amazement, Kevin stole the other team's inbound pass and put away a nifty behind-the-back layup. He finished that night with 43 points and nearly as many highlight film clips.

There was something else about Kevin that was unusual in a young star player. He was completely unselfish. Rather than shoot the ball himself at crucial times, he would often pass off to a teammate, even an inexperienced freshman. Coach Nelson would stand on the sidelines screaming, "Kevin, don't pass! Shoot! Shoot!"

Kevin made a new best friend that year, junior guard Ronnie Fields. Those two players led the Farragut Admirals to a 28–2 record. The team got to the Illinois quarterfinals before bowing out of the state championships. Kevin was the big man, taking care of business under the baskets. Fields was a dazzling small man, with showstopping moves and a forty-seven-inch vertical leap. Together, they were the best show in town. Fields later went on to play in the Continental Basketball Association.

"Kevin and Ronnie—it was like they were rock stars, it was like a circus," Coach Nelson said. "I was talking to sports agents, scouts, coaches, media people. Eighty percent of the calls coming into the school were for me."

At the end of the season, Kevin averaged 25.2 points, 18 rebounds, 6.7 assists, and 6.5 blocked shots per game. He was named National High School Player of the Year by *USA Today*, and Mr. Basketball by the state of Illinois.

Kevin was chosen to play in the McDonald's All-American Game, which features the top two dozen high school players in the country. He was nervous about playing against other top players. How would he hold up? Kevin opened the game with a 360-degree spinning dunk. He then sprinted back on defense and blocked the other team's first shot. By game's end he had 18 points and 11 rebounds. He was named the Most Outstanding Player, an award that had previously gone to future NBA superstars such as Grant Hill, Penny Hardaway, and Shaquille O'Neal.

But while he had a wonderful year on the court, Kevin had problems keeping his grades up in school. Reading had always been a chore for him, and transferring from one high school to another right before his senior year did not make things any easier.

Colleges require that students score well on high school tests if they want to play college sports as freshmen. Kevin took the tests several times but was unable to achieve the score. He was getting frustrated, and his mother was having more difficulty making ends meet. Money was very tight.

Kevin, his mother, and his high school coaches talked for months about his future. Then he made a daring decision. A few days after he turned nineteen, he announced he would not try to go to college. Instead, he would try to go straight to the NBA.

The decision was a risky one. Some people felt that Garnett's biggest problem would be adjusting to adult life at age nineteen. Professional sports may seem like a glamorous career, but it is a grueling lifestyle of traveling from city to city, living in hotels, and dealing with temptations. Garnett had never even lived away from home.

Beyond that was the question of whether he was good enough to compete in the NBA. Being the country's top high school player was one thing. Trying to out-rebound Hakeem Olajuwon, Alonzo Mourning, or Chris Webber was quite

After his stellar senior year at Farragut, Garnett played in the McDonald's All-American game, an annual all-star game showcasing the top high school seniors in the country. The game has featured many future NBA stars.

another. Garnett stood just under seven feet tall, but he was still a string bean, weighing a mere 220 pounds. One good elbow from a strong player such as Charles Barkley, critics said, and he might just wither away.

Until 1974, the NBA had an age rule that kept players out of the league until their college class graduated. But a court decided that this rule was illegal. If a player was good enough, the court said, his age should not matter.

Over the next twenty years, just five players had tried jumping to pro basketball without ever playing in college. Two ended up being washouts. A third, Darryl Dawkins, had some success, although experts said he would have had a better career if he had had some college experience.

There were also two success stories. Moses Malone joined the old American Basketball Association straight from high school in 1974. Over the next two decades, he set rebounding records and won an NBA title with the Philadelphia 76ers. Shawn Kemp enrolled in junior college, but never played there, before joining the Seattle SuperSonics in 1989. He became a many-time All-Star.

Now Garnett would try to make the same jump. He filed for the 1995 NBA Draft and was projected to go anywhere from the fourth pick to the fourteenth. Some teams were afraid of choosing him because of his tender age. But others felt that choosing Garnett could have a tremendous upside. "Get Garnett and you've got an All-Star well into the 21st Century . . . when Michael and Shaq aren't in town. Get Garnett and you're in the Finals two years from now."

But which team? Garnett's first choice was to play for the Toronto Raptors. He had met Raptors general manager Isiah Thomas, and the two men had hit it off. But Garnett realized that players entering the NBA go where they are selected—not necessarily where they want to go. "Wherever I go, it will be

Despite being double-teamed, Garnett beats the Indiana Pacers defenders to the hoop. Many experts felt Garnett was not mentally or physically ready when he decided to skip college and go straight to the NBA.

an opportunity," he said. "Millions of kids want to play pro basketball. Here I am getting the chance early. I learned one thing—never hate a positive option."

On June 26, 1995, the twenty-nine NBA teams gathered at the Toronto SkyDome to choose new players. The Golden State Warriors had the first pick and drafted University of Maryland's Joe Smith, a six-foot ten-inch scorer. The Los Angeles Clippers, with the next pick, selected University of Alabama forward Antonio McDyess. Then the Philadelphia 76ers picked Jerry Stackhouse, a six-foot five-inch swingman from the University of North Carolina. All three players had something in common—each was leaving college early. And each was just twenty years old. It seemed that the NBA teams were going for youth.

The Washington Bullets had the next pick. They needed a big man to cover the middle. Many experts expected them to draft Garnett. But the Bullets instead went for Rasheed Wallace, a lanky center from North Carolina.

The next club up was the Minnesota Timberwolves.

## Chapter 4

NBA Commissioner David Stern rose to the podium at the Toronto SkyDome. "With the fifth pick of the 1995 NBA draft," Stern said, "the Minnesota Timberwolves select, from Farragut Academy in Chicago, Kevin Garnett."

Amid applause, Garnett stood up. He smiled broadly. He was handed a green-and-blue baseball cap with "Wolves" on it. He put it on his head, and his smile grew even wider. Minnesota seemed like a good fit. Sure, the Timberwolves had never made the NBA playoffs during their six-year existence. They had never even come close to finishing a season with a winning record.

Garnett was pleased for two reasons. First, having been raised in a small town in South Carolina, he preferred going to a smaller city, like Minneapolis, rather than to a giant city like New York or Los Angeles. Life would be simpler there, he figured. Second, the Timberwolves had a new general manager who promised to devote himself to building Garnett into an NBA star. A Pro Basketball Hall of Famer, Kevin McHale played thirteen seasons for the Boston Celtics and helped lead them to three NBA championships. Like Garnett, McHale was six feet eleven inches and thin. He was a great rebounder and averaged 18 points per game over his pro career.

Now McHale would become the teacher. Through the summer leading up to Garnett's rookie season, the two men worked together eight hours a day. They hoisted weights to help build up Garnett's body. He would need to be stronger to battle for rebounds against the likes of Patrick Ewing. McHale taught his star student the low-post moves that had worked for him as a pro. Garnett would need those tricks to compete against smart players like David Robinson. And they spent endless hours shooting the ball from different parts of the court. "If Shaquille O'Neal pushes you outside," McHale said, "you had better be able to sink an eighteen-foot jumper."

After each day's session, the two men would go out for dinner. For hours they would talk, about basketball, about other players, about life. Mostly, Garnett asked questions of the older man. "If you don't ask questions," Garnett said, "you'll never learn anything."

By the end of the summer, McHale was impressed. "What the kid has accomplished is amazing," the proud teacher said. "If you put him in a college situation right now, where it's not as physical, he'd be doing things that would have people in awe."

Certainly most people would be in awe of his paycheck. That summer, Garnett signed a three-year contract with the Timberwolves that would pay him $5.6 million. He used his first paycheck to buy his mother a house back in South Carolina. His youngest sister, Ashley, moved in with Kevin in an apartment in downtown Minneapolis. She went to a local high school and starred on the girl's basketball team. Garnett's best childhood buddy, Jaime "Bug" Peters, also moved in.

Unlike some young athletes who spend their money foolishly, Garnett hired experts to help him handle his money. His

Garnett slam dunks over Elliot Perry of the Milwaukee Bucks. The Timberwolves were so impressed with Garnett's raw ability they took him with the fifth pick of the 1995 NBA Draft, even though he was barely nineteen years old.

biggest purchase was a computer, which he used to study the stock market.

Most of his time, of course, was spent studying for his new job. And as excited as Garnett was to start, so were Timberwolves fans about his arrival. They gave him the nickname, Da Kid. One local restaurant even developed the "Da Kid Special"—a mushroom-and-pepper pizza—after learning that it was Garnett's favorite. Each week they sent a few to his apartment.

All the excitement, however, could not help the Wolves on the court. The season opened with two losses, and by early January, the team had just 7 wins and 21 losses. Starting point guard Micheal Williams injured his left heel and was gone for the season. His replacement, rookie Jerome Allen, missed fifteen games because of a bad knee. Head Coach Bill Blair was fired in December and was replaced by Flip Saunders. And two of the team's best players—guard Isaiah Rider and forward Christian Laettner—openly argued over who should shoot the ball more often.

The season was a mess. General Manager McHale knew that building a winner would take time. His biggest concern was that Garnett might get discouraged. In January, McHale went to a team practice and saw his prize rookie's eyes brimming with frustration. At the time, Garnett was struggling. Coming off the bench as a substitute, he was averaging just 6 points and 3 rebounds per game. By all accounts, the numbers were less than everyone had expected.

McHale brought the nineteen-year-old into his office. Then he showed Garnett the rookie statistics of two NBA superstars—Shawn Kemp of the Seattle SuperSonics and Scottie Pippen of the Chicago Bulls. Garnett's eyes widened at the numbers.

"Take a good look," McHale said. "These aren't much different than your numbers. These players have gone on to become stars. The last thing I need is for you to get discouraged. I don't care how good you are. I care how good you will be."

The pep talk worked. Garnett realized that the point of his rookie season was not so much to win as it was to build for the future. Up to that point, he had been afraid of taking too many shots, afraid of missing. Now McHale told him to go out and do the best he could, without worrying about the results.

McHale and Saunders also moved Garnett into the starting lineup. On January 9, 1996, he became the third-youngest player ever to start a game at nineteen years, 235 days. He scored just 9 points against the Los Angeles Lakers that night. But then things started getting better.

A few weeks later, the Wolves and Houston Rockets were tied early in the fourth quarter. Then Garnett took over the game. First he took a pass from teammate Terry Porter. He put a drop-step fake on Rockets center Hakeem Olajuwon and swished a twelve-footer through the net. Then, when Rockets guard Clyde Drexler clanked a jump shot, Garnett hauled down the rebound and went coast-to-coast for a layup. The Rockets tried to regroup, but Garnett stole an inbounds pass from Chucky Brown and slammed home a monster dunk that left the backboard rattling for twenty seconds.

Over a stretch of four minutes, Garnett had 9 straight points, 4 rebounds, and 2 blocked shots. The Timberwolves pulled away for a 110–101 victory.

"This guy has as much energy as anyone I've ever seen," stunned Houston coach Rudy Tomjanovich said after the game. "He attacks the boards like he's in a gym all by himself. The scary part is, he's only 25 percent of what he'll be some day."

The good games continued. In a March game at Philadelphia, Garnett pulled down a team-record 19 rebounds. A few nights later, he scored 33 points against the Boston Celtics.

Kevin Garnett gives Spurs star Tim Duncan a sample of his strong inside play. Minnesota general manager and former Boston Celtics great Kevin McHale taught Garnett the low-post moves that helped make McHale an All-Star.

Against the Chicago Bulls, he snared 12 rebounds and blocked 4 shots—including two by Michael Jordan. Afterward, Garnett grinned from ear to ear when he was told that Jordan had predicted future greatness for him.

Garnett's scoring average was slowly climbing. But it was the other elements of his game—rebounding, shot-blocking, and defense—that impressed his teammates the most.

"Kevin is like Magic Johnson in a way," said Wolves guard James Robinson. "Magic could control a game without scoring a basket. That's the way Kevin is."

In February 1996, Garnett was invited to play in the NBA's rookie All-Star Game in San Antonio, Texas. He enjoyed the chance to hang out with other young stars, like Jerry Stackhouse and Damon Stoudamire. He played well, finishing with 8 points, 6 assists, 4 rebounds, 2 steals, and a block.

He finished the season averaging 10.4 points and 6.3 rebounds. He also averaged 1.64 blocks per game, ranking fifteenth in the NBA. He started 43 of the Wolves' 82 games, mostly in the second half of the season. In those starts, he raised his numbers to 14 points, 8.4 rebounds, and 2.26 blocks per game.

Learning to play the game was one thing. Learning to adjust to life as a pro was another. Garnett would not turn twenty until after his rookie season ended. He was a boy leading a man's life. The eighty-two-game schedule was grueling. The travel, to a different city nearly every night, could be tiresome.

Garnett's oasis was his Minneapolis apartment, where he could escape to his video games and his microwave popcorn, the kinds of things that keep most teenagers going. His younger sister was there to provide a sense of family. Although Garnett was never a great student, he loved helping his sister Ashley with her homework. His best friend, Bug Peters, took

Garnett struggled through the first two months of his rookie season. McHale told him not to get discouraged because many NBA superstars had struggled early in their careers.

care of the bills and the shopping and was always there to lend a supportive ear when Garnett needed one.

"I found out that it's not just accepting the money or the chance to play in the pros," Garnett said. "It's accepting the responsibility of playing in a man's league. Now don't get me wrong. I don't consider myself a grownup yet. But I found out fast, you had better be ready to *act* like a grownup in this league."

His nickname—Da Kid—stuck. But he was earning another nickname—The Franchise. The Timberwolves won just twenty-six games and lost fifty-six during Garnett's rookie season, but they knew they had found the biggest building block for the team's future. Now they just had to find some other pieces to fit around him.

That would come in the fall of 1996. And it would come in the form of an old friend.

## Chapter 5

One July night after his rookie season, Kevin Garnett was back home in South Carolina, munching on French fries and watching the NBA draft on television. The Timberwolves had the fifth pick in the draft. Garnett had just one hope—that they would select his old telephone buddy, Stephon Marbury. In addition to being a long-distance pal, Marbury had been a brilliant point guard at Georgia Tech. He was just what the Wolves needed, Garnett figured.

The Milwaukee Bucks, however, had the pick ahead of Minnesota. When the Bucks chose Marbury, Garnett's heart sank. A few minutes later, the Wolves took another guard, Ray Allen of the University of Connecticut. Okay, Garnett figured, but not as good.

More news came within an hour. Milwaukee and Minnesota had swapped draft picks. The twenty-year-old Marbury was coming to town. He and Garnett would be NBA teammates, as well as soul mates.

"Kevin kept telling me we had to get Stephon," said Timberwolves general manager Kevin McHale. "I told him we'd love to. But we weren't sure [Marbury] was going to be around long enough for us to get a swing at him."

Garnett and Marbury had met in person just twice before. Their friendship had truly been one that covered many miles. They had played only one game together, a pickup contest at a Chicago gym when Garnett was still in high school. Now, two years later, it did not take long for their chemistry to develop further.

In the first game of 1996, Marbury pounded his dribble downcourt. He waited, looking for Garnett to make a move. Other teammates and defenders swirled around. But Marbury waited, trying to catch Garnett's eye. The two exchanged glances, and Marbury winked. With that, Garnett muscled past Los Angeles Clippers forward Bo Outlaw and made his move toward the basket. Marbury lobbed a rainbow pass toward the hoop. Garnett clutched the ball above the rim and stuffed it through. It was the perfect alley-oop.

As the 1996–97 season went on, Garnett and Marbury operated dozens of alley-oops, give-and-go plays, fast-break baskets, and pick-and-rolls. They perfected old-time plays and invented some new ones as well. The Timberwolves, NBA doormats for so long, were winning. And two twenty-year-olds were leading the way.

Throughout NBA history, most winning teams have boasted two great players. It makes sense. Having a second great scorer on your team prevents defenses from triple-teaming your best player. The Los Angeles Lakers of the 1980s had Kareem-Abdul Jabbar in the middle and Magic Johnson in the backcourt. The Chicago Bulls of the 1990s had Michael Jordan and Scottie Pippen, both of whom were great shooters and defensive players. The Utah Jazz rose to the top of the standings mostly through guard John Stockton's great passes to power forward Karl Malone.

During the 1996–97 season, the Timberwolves began to play an exciting brand of basketball. Leading the charge was Garnett, along with rookie point guard Stephon Marbury, and forward Tom Gugliotta.

Could Garnett and Marbury join that elite group? Certainly it was too early to say for sure. But as they began their careers together, the two young friends gave Minnesota fans as much to hope for as any fans in the NBA.

"Talent and friendship is a nice blend," McHale said. "I like that aspect of Kevin and Stephon. These guys play unselfish ball. One guy has a bigger game one night, the other isn't upset. I think you should compete against the other team. That's the way Steph and Kevin think too."

After home games, the two players would go back to Garnett's apartment. They would order take-out pizza—perhaps a "Da Kid Special"—and stay up late watching a video of the game they had just played. Sometimes they would sit at the kitchen table and diagram plays to try in their next game.

Led by the talented twosome, along with high-scoring power forward Tom Gugliotta, the Timberwolves reached mid-season with as many wins as they had losses. Never before had they accomplished that. There was even more exciting news: Garnett, along with forward Tom Gugliotta, was chosen to play in the 1997 All-Star Game in Cleveland's Gund Arena.

Garnett was overwhelmed at being picked to play with the greatest of the greats. He got to meet two of his heroes, NBA legends Wilt Chamberlain and Magic Johnson. He said afterward that he had pinched himself to make sure he was not dreaming. During the two days of practicing before the game, other All-Stars teased him about his age. After all, he was the only guy on the team who could not enter certain restaurants that required customers to be at least twenty-one years old. But along with the teasing came a load of respect for the young phenom.

"I'd much rather have them kid me than not say anything," Garnett said. "I'm just trying to have fun with these knuckleheads, this group of comedians."

Garnett played eighteen minutes in the 1997 NBA All-Star Game. He scored 6 points and grabbed a team-high 9 rebounds for the Western Conference team. On one play, he came down for a rebound battling the Miami Heat's Alonzo Mourning for the ball. Although Mourning outweighed him by forty-five pounds, Garnett ripped the rebound out of the larger man's arms. On another play, he blocked a shot by Reggie Miller of the Indiana Pacers. As the ball was headed out of bounds, Garnett dived and tapped it to a teammate, who headed upcourt on a fast break.

Late in the game, he found himself standing next to David Robinson, the great center for the San Antonio Spurs. "You've got terrific skills," Robinson said. "Keep working."

The youngster patted the former league MVP. Making reference to one of Robinson's television commercials, Garnett said, "Thanks. Someday I want to have my own neighborhood."

It is no mystery why even the greatest NBA veterans have so much respect for this youngster. First there are his skills. At six feet eleven inches tall, Garnett was the league's tallest small forward. That means he has the height and jumping ability to block shots and fight for rebounds. He also has the silky coordination of a point guard. Not many big men can dribble the ball the length of the court without getting it stolen. Garnett does that all the time.

Beyond that, people admire the way Garnett carries himself as a man. Unlike many young athletes, he does not slouch and sneer. He looks people in the eye. He asks strangers their names. He treats people well—from coaches to the janitors who sweep the floor after practice.

He also respects his elders. In his second season, Garnett used almost every game as a learning tool. Before or after the contest he tried to single out one opponent and ask for advice. He asked Charles Barkley, "How do you position yourself for

Kobe Bryant admires a Garnett slam dunk during the 1998 All-Star Game. Garnett made his All-Star Game debut in 1997 and paced the Western Conference team with 9 rebounds.

so many rebounds?" He asked Karl Malone, "How might I build up my body?" He asked Grant Hill, "How can a young player become a team leader?"

"He gets better every night," said Timberwolves assistant coach Doc Rivers, who starred for thirteen seasons in the NBA. "But it's more than that. This kid has style. He's got that Ken Griffey, Jr., charisma. That's something nobody else can teach him. You're either born with it or you're not. And Kevin Garnett was born with it."

The night Rivers said this, the Wolves played the New Jersey Nets. Garnett scored 15 points and grabbed 10 rebounds. He made it look easy. In the second half, he made a move that brought the crowd to its feet. He took a pass from Marbury on the right side of the basket. He went to a left-handed dribble and ducked his head to drive toward the net. Three Nets were now on him. Suddenly, Garnett leaped into the air and twisted around two of the Nets. He dropped a ten-foot jumper through the basket as softly as tossing a coin into a wishing well.

After seven long years in which the Timberwolves had never won more than 29 games, 1996–97 was a breakout season. Minnesota won 40 games, erasing the previous team record by early March. For the first time, the team made the NBA playoffs. The fans, so frustrated over the years, began packing the Target Center for games.

The playoff stay was brief. The Wolves lost out to the Houston Rockets in three straight games. They had nothing to be embarrassed about. The Rockets were among the NBA's top teams. Minnesota was headed in the right direction.

No one, Garnett said, should be surprised by their improvement. "Our future looks bright, and it's all because of hard work and dedication," he said. "Kevin McHale has taught us that we are going to play hard. If we don't play hard, he's going to bring in someone who will. We are loving the game,

Shawn Bradley and the rest of the Dallas Mavericks defense are left in the dust as Garnett goes in for an easy basket. With Garnett and Stephon Marbury leading the way, Minnesota reached the playoffs for the first time in franchise history in 1997.

and that's the biggest thing right now—that we love what we do and put our whole heart into it. I think the difference with our team is the competitiveness. It's been instilled in us to go out and compete at a high level every night. I think Minnesota is the future right now."

The following season, the future would look even better.

## Chapter 6

During the summer of 1997, Kevin Garnett returned home to South Carolina. He wanted to give something back to Mauldin, the town that had helped raise him. He spent $25,000 of his own money to resurface Springfield Park, where he had spent so many hours of his youth shooting hoops.

The night the park reopened, Garnett hosted a free cookout for all his hometown's residents. Every table was decorated with a picture of him, and with cantaloupes sprayed orange to look like basketballs. His high school jersey number—the same number twenty-one that he wears for the Timberwolves—was retired in a ceremony on the high school football field.

"He's not just a great player, he's a great young man," said Mauldin mayor Charles Bankhead. "He comes back here and really pulls together the community."

That summer, Garnett played basketball with high school boys in Mauldin's recreation center every day. Afterward, he would take a dozen or more of them out to eat chicken, fish, and vegetables. He urged the boys to drink lots of juice, not soda.

During the summer of 1997, Garnett returned home to South Carolina and donated $25,000 to resurface Springfield Park, where he honed his basketball skills while growing up.

When everyone pushed back their plates after eating, Garnett told stories about the NBA. The kids asked questions. What was it really like to play against Michael Jordan? Was Dennis Rodman as crazy as he seemed?

On Friday nights the group, including some young coaches, would talk of going to a movie. Then someone would ask Garnett what he wanted to do. "What he wanted to do was go play basketball," said Chris Garrett, a Mauldin High assistant. "So, we'd always play more basketball."

Kevin Garnett could not get enough of the game—whether he was playing with NBA All-Stars or with teenagers at the local gym. His love for the sport, and his dedication to it, were helping to turn him into one of basketball's top stars.

Garnett turned in a brilliant all-around season in 1997–98. He was the only player in the NBA to finish among the top twenty-five players in five separate categories—points, rebounds, assists, blocks, and steals. He started all eighty-two Timberwolves games. He set franchise records in nearly every category.

Most superstars in sports excel in a few areas. Mark McGwire is baseball's home run king—but don't ask him to steal a base. For years, Barry Sanders was the NFL's most elusive runner—but he often sat when a power run was called for. The same is true in basketball. You rarely see giant Shaquille O'Neal trying a long-distance three-pointer. And it would not be fair to ask a sleek guard like Allen Iverson to crash the boards for a clutch rebound.

Garnett, on the other hand, is a rare breed. He can play inside and outside. He is tall enough to fight for rebounds, but quick enough to snatch the ball from your hands. If a situation calls for power, he has it. If it calls for speed, he has that, too.

"He is the total package," said Michael Jordan. "He has come a long way, and you know what's scary about it? He's

Garnett is said to possess a good inside/outside game. This means that he is able to score and defend from practically anywhere on the court.

still got a long way to come. You're just seeing a touch of his skills. I'll just say this: Everyone had better be aware of the Wolves in the coming years."

If the NBA was not already aware, it became so in 1997–98. The Wolves lost fourteen of their first twenty-five games. Then they turned it around to win fourteen of their next sixteen. By season's end, they were 45–37. For the first time in its eight seasons, Minnesota had a winning record.

One of the key turnaround games came on December 30, 1997, against Jordan's Chicago Bulls. Up until then, the Wolves had never beaten Chicago, losing sixteen straight. But that night, Garnett nearly single-handedly put an end to the losing streak.

With the Wolves down by five in the third quarter, Garnett picked the pocket of Bulls guard Steve Kerr. He drove past Rodman for a layup—forcing a foul for good measure. A minute later, Garnett blocked a shot by Jordan and tossed a floor-length pass to teammate Tom Gugliotta for an easy two points. And on the next drive down the court, Garnett reached over Rodman to grab a missed shot by teammate Terry Porter. He stuffed it through the rim. Rodman shook his head in disbelief.

In the space of two minutes, Garnett had wowed the crowd with all his skills—defense, passing, shooting, rebounding, and shot-blocking—and with his power and speed. In the process, the Wolves beat the Bulls, 99–95, for the first time in history. A corner had been turned in Minnesota. Kevin Garnett, just twenty-one years old, had shown his teammates they could beat anyone.

It was not just teammates and opponents who saw how good Garnett was becoming. The NBA's fans recognized it, too. In February 1998, they voted him as a Western Conference starter in the All-Star Game.

When Garnett went to Madison Square Garden in New

Garnett shoots a long-range bomb over the outstretched arms of Boston's Todd Day.

York City, he noticed that some of the other All-Stars seemed almost bored to be there. Maybe they had been to so many All-Star Games that it was no big deal to them. Certainly, Garnett did not feel that way. "People who say they get tired of playing in the All-Star Game probably don't cherish it like I do," he told reporters. "I mean, how many kids dream of playing in the NBA? I'll always have the mindset to be thankful because I know a lot of guys don't make it. And when you get voted in, it shows how much the fans think of you. I can never take that for granted."

Garnett played just under half the game. He finished with 12 points, 4 rebounds, 2 assists, 2 steals, and 1 block. In one memorable play, he took a pass along the baseline and found himself covered by Glen Rice of the Charlotte Hornets. He dribbled with his left hand, daring Rice to try to steal the ball. When Rice went for it, Garnett flipped it into his right hand. He launched a ten-foot jumper, as Rice hit the ground in frustration.

After his first All-Star Game in Cleveland the year before, Garnett had taken home nothing more than a few chocolate chip cookies that he scooped up in the postgame interview room. This time, when the game ended, he found himself holding the game ball. He took it home as a memory of his first All-Star start.

Garnett and his young teammates learned a lot of lessons that season. One was that there is no room for fear in the NBA. After the most successful regular season in their history, the Timberwolves advanced to the playoffs against the Seattle SuperSonics. Seattle's all-time record against Minnesota stood at 32–4. The Sonics won Game 1 by fifteen points, but the Wolves stayed poised. Two days later, Minnesota posted a 98–93 shocker at Seattle, then returned home to the Target Center for a 98–90 win. The wins were the first postseason victories in the history of the franchise.

In the 1997–98 season, the Timberwolves went 45–37. It was the first time in franchise history that they finished the season with a winning record.

Of course, another lesson is that there is always more to learn. Seattle, the more experienced team, came back to win the series in five games. The Wolves were not ready yet. But they were getting better.

How would that play out their following year? Unfortunately, the Wolves' momentum got sidetracked. A dispute between the NBA's owners and players—partly centered on Garnett's giant contract—shut down the league for two months. When they got back to playing, the Wolves made trades that completely shook up the team. They sent Gugliotta to the Phoenix Suns. Then, Garnett's longtime friend, Stephon Marbury, was traded to the New Jersey Nets.

"It hurts, because I've always loved Stephon, as a teammate and as a buddy," Garnett said. "But playing pro basketball is a business. In business, people come and people go, and it isn't always what you would like to see happen. But you have to keep working as hard as you can."

Kevin Garnett kept working hard in 1999. In the shortened NBA season, he became a dominant player. He finished ninth in the NBA in rebounding (10.4 per game), and eleventh in scoring (20.8 points per game). Again, he was chosen to play in the All-Star Game, and picked up more tips from great veteran players.

The Wolves finished the season with 25 wins and 25 losses. In the 50 games, Garnett led his team in scoring 34 times and rebounding 37 times. The Wolves lost to the San Antonio Spurs, three games to one, in the playoffs. Garnett was disappointed, but took some pride in the fact that the Spurs were the eventual 1999 NBA champions. There was no shame in losing to the champion.

Besides, there was always a fine future to look forward to. Perhaps, Garnett thought, he would someday play for a champion.

## Career Statistics

| YEAR | TEAM | GP | FG% | REB | AST | STL | BLK | PTS | RPG | PPG |
|---|---|---|---|---|---|---|---|---|---|---|
| 1995–96 | Minnesota | 80 | .491 | 501 | 145 | 86 | 131 | 835 | 6.3 | 10.4 |
| 1996–97 | Minnesota | 77 | .499 | 618 | 236 | 105 | 163 | 1,309 | 8.0 | 17.0 |
| 1997–98 | Minnesota | 82 | .491 | 786 | 348 | 139 | 150 | 1,518 | 9.6 | 18.5 |
| 1998–99 | Minnesota | 47 | .460 | 489 | 202 | 78 | 83 | 977 | 10.4 | 20.8 |
| *Totals* | | 286 | .486 | 2,394 | 931 | 408 | 527 | 4,639 | 8.4 | 16.2 |

**GP**=Games Played
**FG%**=Field Goal Percentage
**REB**=Rebounds
**AST**=Assists
**STL**=Steals
**BLK**=Blocks
**PTS**=Points
**RPG**=Rebounds per game
**PPG**=Points per game

## *Where to Write Kevin Garnett:*

Mr. Kevin Garnett
c/o Minnesota Timberwolves
Target Center
600 First Avenue North
Minneapolis, MN 55403

## *On the Internet at:*

http://www.nba.com/playerfile/kevin_garnett.html
http://www.nba.com/timberwolves

# *Index*

**A**
Abdul-Jabbar, Kareem, 44
Allen, Jerome, 37
Allen, Ray, 43
Amateur Athletic Union, 19
American Basketball Association, 31

**B**
Bankhead, Charles, 52
Barkley, Charles, 7, 10, 31, 47
Blair, Bill, 37
Boston Celtics, 34, 38
Brown, Chucky, 38

**C**
Chamberlain, Wilt, 13, 46
Charlotte Hornets, 58
Chicago Bulls, 37, 40, 44, 56
Chicago Medical Center, 25
Continental Basketball Association, 28

**D**
Dawkins, Darryl, 31
Drexler, Clyde, 38

**E**
ESPN Television, 24
Ewing, Patrick, 35

**F**
Farragut (Illinois) Academy, 25–26, 28
Fields, Ronnie, 28
Fisher, Duke, 17, 19
Franks, Baron, 17

**G**
Garnett, Ashley, 25, 35, 40
Garnett, Shirley, 16, 24
Garrett, Chris, 54
Gazaway, Darren, 19–20
Georgia Tech, 43
Golden State Warriors, 33
Griffey, Ken, Jr., 49
Gugliotta, Tom, 46, 56, 60
Gund Arena, 46

**H**
Hardaway, Penny, 13, 29
Hill, Grant, 29, 49
Houston Rockets, 38, 49

**I**
Indiana Pacers, 47
Irby, Ernest, 16
Iverson, Allen, 54

**J**
Johnson, Magic, 10, 11, 13, 40, 44, 46
Jordan, Michael, 11, 40, 44, 54, 56

**K**
Kemp, Shawn, 31, 37
Kerr, Steve, 56

**L**
Laettner, Christian, 37
Long, Murray, 22
Los Angeles Clippers, 33, 44
Los Angeles Lakers, 38, 44

**M**
Madison Square Garden, 11, 56
Malone, Karl, 44, 49
Malone, Moses, 31
Manning, Danny, 7, 9
Marbury, Stephon, 22, 24, 26, 43–44, 46, 49, 60
Marcello, Seven-Gun, 26
Mauldin (South Carolina) High School, 17, 20, 22, 25, 54
McCullough, O'Lewis, 17

McDonald's All-American Game, 28
McDyess, Antonio, 33
McGwire, Mark, 54
McHale, Kevin, 10, 34–35, 37–38, 43, 46, 49
Miami Heat, 47
Miller, Reggie, 47
Milwaukee Bucks, 43
Mr. Basketball (Illinois), 28
Mourning, Alonzo, 29, 47
Mutombo, Dikembe, 13

**N**

NBA All-Star Game, 11, 46–47, 56, 58
NBA Draft, 31, 33–34
Nelson, William, 25, 28
New Jersey Nets, 49, 60
*Nightline*, 22

**O**

Olajuwon, Hakeem, 29, 38
O'Neal, Shaquille, 13, 29, 35
Outlaw, Bo, 44

**P**

Peters, Jaime "Bug," 22, 35, 40
Philadelphia 76ers, 31, 33
Phoenix Suns, 7, 9, 60
Pippen, Scottie, 37, 44
Porter, Terry, 38, 56

**R**

Rice, Glen, 58
Rider, Isaiah, 37
Rivers, Doc, 49

Robinson, David, 13, 35, 47
Robinson, James, 40
Rodman, Dennis, 54, 56

**S**

San Antonio Spurs, 13, 47
Sanders, Barry, 54
Saunders, Flip, 13, 37
Seattle SuperSonics, 31, 37, 58
*Slam* Magazine, 24
Smith, Joe, 33
Stackhouse, Jerry, 33, 40
Stern, David, 34
Stockton, John, 44
Stoudamire, Damon, 40

**T**

Target Center, 49, 58
Thomas, Isiah, 31
Tomjanovich, Rudy, 38
Toronto Raptors, 31
Toronto Skydome, 33–34

**U**

University of Alabama, 33
University of Connecticut, 43
University of Maryland, 33
University of North Carolina, 33
*USA Today*, 28
Utah Jazz, 44

**W**

Wallace, Rasheed, 33
Washington Bullets, 33
Webber, Chris, 13, 29
Williams, Micheal, 37
Willoughby, Janie, 20